A JIGSAW JONES MYSTERY®

Jigsaw Jones' Detective Tips

Based on the mysteries
by James Preller
illustrated by Jamie Smith
cover illustration by R. W. Alley

A
LITTLE APPLE
PAPERBACK

SCHOLASTIC INC.
New York Toronto London Auckland Sydney
Mexico City New Delhi Hong Kong Buenos Aires

ISBN 0-439-79397-1

Special thanks to Robin Wasserman

12 11 10 9 8 7 6 5 4 3 2 1 6 7 8 9 10 11/0

Printed in the U.S.A. 40
First printing, February 2006

Introduction

Do you have what it takes to be a detective like Jigsaw Jones?

Well, that depends. Do you love solving puzzles and secret codes? Do you pay attention to details and notice things that other people miss? Are you creative? Clever? Brave? Do you have a best friend who can help you every step of the way?

Congratulations! It sounds like you have everything you need to start solving cases.

What did you say?

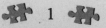

You still don't know *how* to be a detective?

No problem. You see, Jigsaw Jones and Mila Yeh have had a lot of free time on their hands lately. That's the life of a detective. Sometimes you're out solving cases and saving the world from bicycle thieves and brownie-snatchers. Sometimes you're sitting around your office, not doing much of anything.

But Jigsaw and Mila got kind of bored hanging around the office, waiting for the next case to show up. So they decided to take on the biggest mystery of all: how to turn an ordinary kid like you into a **top detective**. They stuffed all their best tips, tricks, and top secret tactics into this book, just for you. Inside, you will learn how to solve cases from start to finish. You will interview witnesses, find fingerprints, spy on suspects, and send messages in secret code, just like a real detective! Once you have all the right moves, you will be able to help Jigsaw and Mila solve a few of their toughest cases. And then you'll be ready to solve some cases of your own.

So let's hurry up and get started — the world is waiting!

Handy How-To Guide

The Who, What, Where, When, and Why's of Being a Detective

Before you solve your first official case, there's a lot you need to know. This section is packed with tons of useful tips so that you can act and sound like a real detective. You'll find out how to set up your detective business . . . and what to do next! Being a detective takes hard work.

Jigsaw's teacher, Ms. Gleason, once said that an inventor only needs three things:

CURIOSITY

IMAGINATION

HARD WORK

Those are the most important tools for a detective, too. And you have them all! But that's just the beginning. Jigsaw and Mila will show you how to use those tools to become the *best* detective in town!

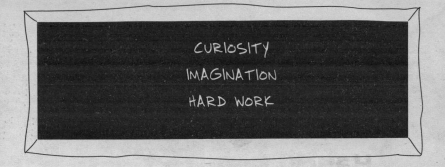

Talk the Talk

If you're going to be a detective, you want to *sound* like a detective, right? That will make your clients trust you. (Plus, it's pretty cool, too.) Here are some key words to help you talk the talk:

Observation: This is the most important thing detectives do. Observation means paying attention to *everything,* even if it doesn't seem important at the time. You never know what could be a clue!

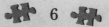

Clue: This is anything that might help you solve a case. It can be a note, a footstep, a fingerprint, or even just a word. The biggest lesson to learn as a detective is that *anything* can be a clue.

Witness: A person who saw what happened is called a witness. Sometimes that's all you need to solve a mystery. But sometimes it just makes you more confused. Because don't forget — people see what they want to see, not always exactly what happened!

Suspect: This is the person who you think might have done something wrong. When Jigsaw and Mila take on a new case, one of the first things they do is make a list of all the possible suspects. Then they try to figure out which suspect really did it.

Motive: A motive is the reason *why* a person did something. In *The Case of the Bear Scare*, Stringbean Noonan pretended there was a bear because he wanted to make friends with a TV star. That was his motive. Coming up with a motive can help you narrow down your list of suspects.

Stakeout: Sometimes you want to catch a suspect in the act. A stakeout is a good way to do that. All you need are a secret hiding place and a lot of patience. Then you wait . . . and wait . . . and wait for your suspect to appear. It's a good idea to bring along some snacks — a stakeout can make you hungry.

Undercover: If you want to catch a suspect without hiding, you can go undercover. That's like hiding in plain sight by wearing a costume or pretending to be someone else. In *The Case of the Detective in Disguise*, Jigsaw went undercover to catch a thief. He put on an apron and carried around a broom, but he was really acting like a bodyguard for a plate of brownies.

You're in Business!

If you're going to be a detective, you might want to make some business cards. That's how Jigsaw and Mila get new clients. Their cards look like this:

NEED A MYSTERY SOLVED?
Call Jigsaw Jones
or Mila Yeh!
For a dollar a day,
we make problems go away.

CALL 555-4523 or 555-4374

(Mila made them. She has better handwriting than Jigsaw.)

What will your business card look like?

There's nothing like a good motto to attract customers. Jigsaw and Mila use "For a dollar a day, we make problems go away." But that wasn't the first idea they came up with. It was just the best one. Here are some of the mottos they decided *not* to use:

Put on a happy face, and we'll solve your case!

Pay us a dollar, or we'll holler!

We solve mysteries. Really.

Your problem is our pleasure!

If you pay, we'll fix your day!

What should your motto be?

Idea #1: ______________________________

Idea #2: ______________________________

Idea #3: ______________________________

Home Sweet Home

The next thing you'll need is an office. Jigsaw and Mila use Jigsaw's tree house. It's big, it's private — and it's close enough to Jigsaw's house for them to grab some cookies when they're hungry. You can use any place you want for your detective's office. You just need room to talk to your clients and to store all of your detective supplies. Here are some of the things that Jigsaw and Mila keep in their office:

Walkie-talkies
Decoder rings
Fingerprint kits
How-to books
Wigs, clothes, and makeup for disguises
Binoculars
Case notebook

My office will be at: ______________________

My must-have equipment:

____

____

____

____

____

____

____

____

____

On the Case

Every time Jigsaw Jones gets a new case, the first thing he does is pull out his detective notebook. Here's what each entry looks like:

The case of: ______________________

Client: ______________________

Suspects: ______________________

Clues: ______________________

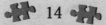

Key words: ________________________________

____

Mystery solved: ________________________________

____

Jigsaw thinks the detective notebook is the most important tool a detective has. He writes down all the information he finds while he's working on a case. Sometimes seeing everything written down in one place can make it a lot easier to solve the puzzle!

The Five W's

When you get a really tough case, it's hard to know where to start looking for answers. When that happens, it can help to write down five basic questions:

Who?

What?

Where?

When?

Why?

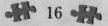

Asking the right questions can lead you to the right answers. And if you can find the right answers to the five W's, you can almost always solve the case!

Try it yourself with *The Case of the Disappearing Cupcake:* Jigsaw had been waiting all morning for lunchtime, because he had a special treat waiting for him. His father had packed him a double-fudge chocolate cupcake with cream filling. At lunchtime, Jigsaw put the cupcake on the table. It looked delicious. Everyone at the table — Mila Yeh, Geetha Nair, Athena Lorenzo, and Bobby Solofsky — said so. Before Jigsaw started eating, he got up to get a napkin. And when he came back, the cupcake was gone!

If *you* were the detective on the case, how would you figure out who took the cupcake? What are some of the *W* questions you could ask?

Who ____________________________________?

What ___________________________________?

Where __________________________________?

When ___________________________________?

Why ____________________________________?

Are there any questions you can answer even *before* you start your investigation?

Mind Reader

One thing you might need to do as a detective is learn to think like your suspects. That means asking yourself things like: Where would *I* have hidden the bicycle if *I* were the thief? Why would *I* have started a food fight? If *I* were Bobby Solofsky, where would *I* stash the stolen cupcake?

In *The Case of the Frog-jumping Contest,* Jigsaw had to think like a *frog*. He had to creep through the slimy, wet swamp grass at night.

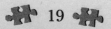

He even tried pretending he liked to eat bugs and say "ribbit." But don't worry. Lucky for you, most of your suspects will probably be human.

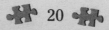

Here's a way for you to practice thinking like someone else. Have a friend or family member write down the answers to these questions. (Helpful hint: The better you know a person, the easier it is to know what they're thinking.)

1. If you could have anything for dinner tonight, what would it be?
2. What is your favorite number?
3. Where would you hide something if you wanted to make sure no one would find it?
4. Who is the person you trust the most?
5. What is your favorite way to spend an afternoon?

Now, without looking at their answers, see if you can figure out what they wrote!

Liar, Liar, Pants on Fire

The truth is, asking questions won't always lead you to the right answers. A detective learns pretty quickly that not everyone tells the truth, the whole truth, and nothing but the truth. So an ace detective needs to be pretty good at spotting a lie, too.

How do you know if you're not getting the real story? Look for clues, of course! Your suspect *might* be lying if he or she:

- won't look you in the eye
- keeps touching his mouth as he talks
- breaks out in a sweat, even if it's cold
- smiles or giggles for no particular reason
- can't stop fidgeting
- talks quickly and offers more details than you need
- mixes up the details or gives you a slightly different answer each time you ask the same question
- crosses his arms
- mumbles

Just remember, even if you're pretty sure someone is lying, you might be wrong. You don't want to accuse your suspect. Just keep asking questions and tracking down clues. Eventually, you'll uncover the truth!

Test Your Detective Skills!

Good detectives like Jigsaw Jones have to pay close attention to everything that goes on around them. This is called being observant. Are you ready to practice your powers of observation?

Before you read the questions below, turn to page 26. Look at the picture for fifteen seconds. Ask a friend or family member to time you. Then see if you can answer the questions below. But don't look back at the picture. That would be cheating!

1. How many people are in the picture?

____

2. Is Jigsaw standing to the right or the left of the store clerk? ______________

3. Is Jigsaw wearing a backpack? ______

4. Describe the person standing behind the counter. ______________________

____

5. How many tables are in the picture?

____

The Scientific Method

According to Jigsaw's teacher, Ms. Gleason, the world is full of mysteries. Scientists try to discover the truth. They ask questions. They investigate. They try to learn facts. Sound familiar? That's right, a scientist is just like a detective! They solve their cases using the *scientific method.* And now you can, too:

1. Identify the problem. *What do you want to know?*

2. Gather information. *What do you already know?*
3. Make a prediction. *What do you think will happen?*
4. Test the prediction. *Experiment!*
5. Draw a conclusion based on what you learned. *Why did the experiment work out the way it did?*

What You See Is(n't) What You Get

Witnesses are funny. They can be wrong even when they are sure they are right. Sometimes two witnesses will disagree about what they saw. One might say a robber wore a mustache and a blue hat. The other might claim the robber had a ponytail and a red hat. Which one is lying? Neither of them. In the confusion, their eyes might play tricks on them.

Your eyes play tricks on you all the time. For example:

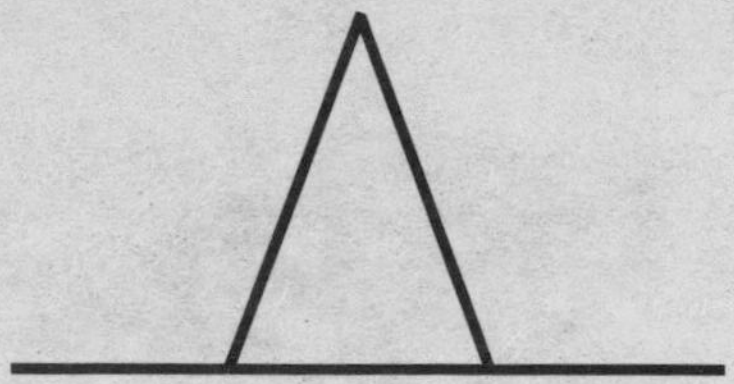

What do you see? Is it a triangle on top of a line? A sailboat on the ocean? A witch's hat? Your eyes see what they want to see.

How about this? Look at it one way and you see a vase. But now look at it differently — can you see two people staring at each other?

Try this one. Look at the note on the next page, and read it as quickly as you can:

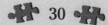

What do you think it says? Did you notice that there is an extra "the"? Most people don't notice it, because they already think they know what it says.

See-and-Spy

Sometimes a detective has to be able to see and hear what's going on without getting caught in the act. In *The Case of the Secret Valentine,* Jigsaw used a See-and-Spy magazine to spy on his family. Now you can make your own See-and-Spy magazine! You may want a grown-up to help you with this project. You'll need:

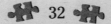

- Newspaper
- A magazine
- Glue
- Wet paper towels
- Tape
- Scissors
- A small mirror

1. First lay out the newspaper so the table doesn't get sticky.
2. Then open the magazine to the inside back cover. Squirt a few globs of glue on the page. This way, it looks like you're reading a page of the magazine, instead of looking at the inside back cover.
3. Next smush the last page of the magazine to the inside back cover. Glue might leak out the edges. Use the wet paper towels to wipe it up.
4. Wait for the glue to dry. Then cut a peephole the size of a quarter into the page of the magazine you just glued.

5. On the opposite page, tape a small mirror to the magazine.
6. Congratulations! You have finished your See-and-Spy magazine! Now sit down and hold the magazine up in front of your face. Pretend to read. You can peek through the hole to see what is happening in front of you. To see what is happening behind you, look in the mirror.

Quick-Draw Artist

Jigsaw loves to draw. He does it for fun, but it also helps him to solve cases. Now you can use drawings in your detective work, too. Every good detective knows that you can tell a lot from the scene of the crime. A good way to start is by drawing a map of the crime scene in your case notebook. To practice, just pick a room in your house. This will be your "crime scene."

First draw an outline of the room. Is it a square? A rectangle? A circle?

Next measure the room. How long is each

wall? How wide is it across? You can use a tape measure, if you have one. But if you don't, you can use your own two feet. Just walk along the wall, heel to toe. Count how many footsteps long each wall is.

Now mark down all the furniture in the room. It doesn't need to look like the actual furniture. You just want to write down what is there and where it is.

Finally, make a list of all the other objects in the room and where they are. Label them on your map. Don't forget to pay attention to all the little details. Remember, *anything* can be a clue!

Face Facts

Making a map isn't the only way to use drawing in your detective work. You can also use sketches to help find a suspect. If you have a witness, he or she can tell you what the suspect looked like. If you draw what they describe, you will have a picture of the suspect. Then someone might recognize the person and solve your case!

Can you be a sketch artist? Find someone to pretend to be your "witness." The witness should think of someone you both know. This will be the "suspect." Now get out your notebook and start asking questions about the suspect. Here are some suggestions:

- Is it a boy or a girl?
- How old is the person?
- What color hair does the person have?
- What color eyes does the person have?
- Is the person's hair long or short? Straight or curly?
- Is the person's nose crooked or straight?
- Does he have a mustache? A beard?
- How much do the person's ears stick out?
- Does the person wear glasses?
- What shape is the person's face? Round? Or long and thin?

As your witness describes the suspect, try drawing the suspect's face. Keep asking questions as you draw, like "Is his hair shorter than this?" "Was his nose bigger or smaller than this?" Don't be afraid to make changes as you go along. (Use a pencil with a big eraser!)

Can you recognize the person your witness is describing?

Riddle Me This

A mystery can be a lot like a riddle. Can you figure out the answers to the riddles on the next page? Here's a clue: In *The Case of Hermie the Missing Hamster,* Jigsaw used a substitution code to read a secret message from Mila. Go to page 53 to find out how the substitution code works. Then you can use the same substitution code to read the answers to the following riddles. Check your answers on the bottom of the next page.

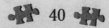

What clothing does a house wear?
1-4-4-18-5-19-19

What gets wetter the more it dries?
1 20-15-23-5-12

What can you catch but not throw?
1 3-15-12-4

Answers: address; a towel; a cold

Invisible Ink

Sometimes ace detectives need to send top secret messages to each other. Jigsaw and Mila used invisible ink messages when they solved *The Case of the Class Clown.* Here's how you can send top secret messages using invisible ink. You'll need:

A paintbrush
Lemon juice
A piece of paper
Water
Iodine

1. First dip a paintbrush in lemon juice. Use it to write a message on a piece of paper.
2. Next, pass the message to your partner.

To read the invisible note:

1. First ask an adult to help mix a jar of water with a few drops of iodine.
2. Then all your partner has to do is brush the water-and-iodine mixture onto the paper. The message will magically appear!

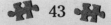

Mirror, Mirror on the Wall

Mirror writing is another fun, simple way to send secret messages. Since the writing is backwards, it's hard to read without looking at it in a mirror. In *The Case of the Christmas Snowman,* Jigsaw sent a mirror message to Mila. Here's how you can send a mirror message to a friend:

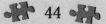

1. Get two sheets of paper. Then write your message on one sheet.
2. Now comes the tricky part. Turn the page over and tape another sheet on

top. Then hold the paper up to a window and copy the message backward.

3. Next remove the first sheet. Now you have a mirror message! To read it, just hold the paper up in front of a mirror.

DESTROY THIS MESSAGE!

— JIGSAW

Leave Your Mark

Whenever you touch an object, you leave something behind: fingerprints. And everyone's fingerprints are *unique*. That means every single person in the world has different fingerprints. And *that* means a good detective can use fingerprints to track down a suspect.

Here's how you can take someone's fingerprints. You'll need:

a scrap of paper

a pencil

a piece of wide, clear tape
a white piece of paper

1. Rub a pencil on a scrap of paper to make a dark smear.
2. Slide your finger back and forth on the smear.
3. Stick a piece of wide, clear tape around your finger.
4. Press your finger (tape side down) on your desk. Be careful not to move it around — you don't want to smudge the pencil.
5. Peel off the tape and stick it onto a white piece of paper. There's your fingerprint!

Try fingerprinting some of your friends. If you have an inkpad, you can use that instead. Label each print with each person's name. Now compare them. Do they all look the same, or do you see differences?

Test yourself! Close your eyes while one of your friends leaves a fingerprint on a piece of paper. Now compare that print to the ones you labeled. Can you figure out who left the print?

Listen Up

Observation isn't just about looking. It can also be about *listening*. You never know what people are saying when they think they are alone. A good detective can hear a lot without being seen. And all you need is a simple drinking glass! Here's what to do:

1. Get two friends or family members to stand in a room. Ask them to take five giant steps away from the door.
2. Then leave the room and shut the door. Have them face the door and talk to each other. No shouting. No whispering.
3. Now place the open end of the glass against the door.
4. Press your ear against the bottom of the glass. What do you hear?

WARNING: Don't use this trick to spy on your parents or your brothers and sisters! It can get you into big trouble! (Just ask Jigsaw.)

Top Secret

Coding and Decoding for the Ace Detective

A good detective needs a good partner. And partners have to be able to send top secret messages to each other. Jigsaw and Mila write to each other in code all the time. When their notes fall into the wrong hands, it doesn't matter, because no one but Jigsaw and Mila can break the code.

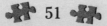

Most codes look hard at first, but they're easy if you know the trick. And lucky for you, Jigsaw and Mila are letting you in on the secret. In fact, they're letting you in on *all* the secrets! Starting on page 53, you'll find all the secret codes you need to help you and your partner crack your cases.

REMEMBER: Always destroy secret messages after you read them. That way they stay secret!

Substitution Code

This is one of the most basic codes. Each number stands for a letter in the alphabet. Number one is the letter A. Number two is the letter B. Number three is the letter C, and so on. To write or decode a message, start by writing down your key:

A	**B**	**C**	**D**	**E**	**F**	**G**	**H**	**I**	**J**	**K**	**L**	**M**
1	2	3	4	5	6	7	8	9	10	11	12	13

N	**O**	**P**	**Q**	**R**	**S**	**T**	**U**	**V**	**W**	**X**	**Y**	**Z**
14	15	16	17	18	19	20	21	22	23	24	25	26

A *key* is what you use to decode a secret message. It tells you how the letters or numbers in your secret code match up to the letters of the actual message.

Now you can decode Jigsaw's message to Mila:

9 19-15-12-22-5-4 20-8-5 13-25-19-20-5-18-25!

Answer: ______________________________

Answer: I solved the mystery!

Combination Code

If you have a combination lock, you can use a reverse substitution code to write down the combination. Write down your substitution code key. In this code, every *letter* stands for a *number.* So if your combination was 25-5-13, you would write:

L-Y, R-E, L-M

"L" and "R" tell you which way to turn the lock. And "Y," "E," and "M" give you the numbers to turn to. Left 25, Right 5, Left 13 — and you've opened the lock!

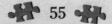

Pig Latin

Pig Latin can be tricky at first. But once you get the hang of it, it's not hard. A lot of kids know a little bit of pig Latin. But if you speak it very fast, most people don't know what you're talking about. With pig Latin, if a word begins with a vowel, you add WAY at the end. So "out" becomes "outway" and "on" becomes "onway." But if a word begins with a consonant, you move the first letter to the end of the word and add AY. So "man" becomes "anmay" and "good" becomes "oodgay."

In pig Latin, Jigsaw Jones is IGSAWJAY ONESJAY.

In pig Latin, my name is ______________

____

Try switching these words to pig Latin:

Detective: ______________________

Mystery: ______________________

Case: ______________________

Partner: ______________________

Weather Code

In a weather code, the only words that matter are the ones that come right after a weather word. So to decode the secret message, just circle all the weather words. Then underline all the words that come next. The underlined words make up your secret message:

ORANGE SAILBOATS RAIN DID FAR AWAY WINDY YOU CAN ALWAYS BREEZY FIGURE SOMETHING HAIL IT IF YOU SUNSHINE OUT?

Answer: ______________________________

Answer: Did you figure it out?

Use the weather code to figure out the secret question written below:

HELP SNOW HOW DID LOVE BLIZZARD MANY IF HE HAIL BROTHERS HOT DOES ZOO MONKEY TABLE CHILLY JIGSAW BOOK PHONE SUMMER HAVE?

Answer: ______________________________

Answer: How many brothers does Jigsaw have?

Do you know the answer?

Answer: ______________________________

Answer: Three

Color Code

This code is sort of like the weather code. Except instead of weather words, you're looking for color words. So just remember, only words that come right after color words matter. You can ignore everything else. Here's another secret question for you:

LUNCH SAILBOAT YELLOW WHO COMPUTER BIG A STOLEN WHITE IS SLEEPY ANGRY DOPEY BLUE JIGSAW'S JOKE MYSTERY TODAY WHY RED TEACHER?

Answer: ________________________________

Answer: Who is Jigsaw's teacher?

Do you know the answer?

Answer: ________________________________

Answer: Ms. Gleason.

Double Backward Code

Jigsaw gets a lot of his codes out of books. But he invented this one himself! First write the letters for each word in reverse order. Then put all the words in reverse order. So if you wanted to write THE CAT ATE, you would write ETA TAC EHT.

Use the double backward code here!

What did the sock say to the foot?

NO EM GNITTUP ERA UOY

Answer: ______________________

Answer: You are putting me on

Jigsaw Code

When Jigsaw Jones needs to think, he does jigsaw puzzles. Puzzles are like solving mysteries. Each piece is a clue. You can practice your skills by sending your partner a secret message through a jigsaw puzzle.

Take a blank piece of paper and write your message in big, thick block letters. Then draw a bunch of squiggly lines crisscrossing the page, as if it were a jigsaw puzzle. Cut across the lines. Your secret message is now a pile of jigsaw pieces. Put them all into an envelope and pass them on!

Alternate Letter Code

This one is pretty easy to read, once you know the trick. You just have to cross out every other letter. Your message is everything that's left!

DJISDL YEOWUK SQOMLCVEEL TEHWEC CLAXSSEJ YLEITQ?

Answer: ______________________________

Answer: Did you solve the case yet?

Zigzag Code

In a zigzag code, the words are written up and down on two lines. You just have to read from top to bottom in each column. Start at the far left. The tricky part is that there are no spaces between each word, so you have to figure that part out yourself!

C N O S L E Y Y T R C D
A Y U O V M M S E Y O E

Answer: ______________________________

Answer: Can you solve my mystery code?

Which case was Jigsaw solving when he used the zigzag code?

T E A E F H D T C I E N I G I E
H C S O T E E E T V I D S U S

Answer: ______________________

Answer: The Case of the Detective in Disguise

Checkerboard Code

To decipher this code, draw a square with twenty-five boxes. Then fill in the letters and number the rows and columns like this:

Column	1	2	3	4	5
Row 1	A	B	C	D	E
Row 2	F	G	H	I	J
Row 3	K	L	M	N	O
Row 4	P	Q	R	S	T
Row 5	U	V	W	X	Y/Z

To make the code, just change each letter into a two-figure number. So to make the letter I, for example, you would write 24. The 2 stands for row 2. The 4 means column number 4.

You can practice by decoding this question:

53-23-35 24-44 25-24-22-44-11-53'44 12-24-22-22-15-44-45 43-24-52-11-32?

Answer: ______________________________

Answer: Who is Jigsaw's biggest rival?

Do you know the answer?

Answer: ______________________________

Answer: Bobby Solofsky

Telephone Code

To solve this code, first draw nine boxes, like the buttons on a telephone. Cross out the Q and the Z.

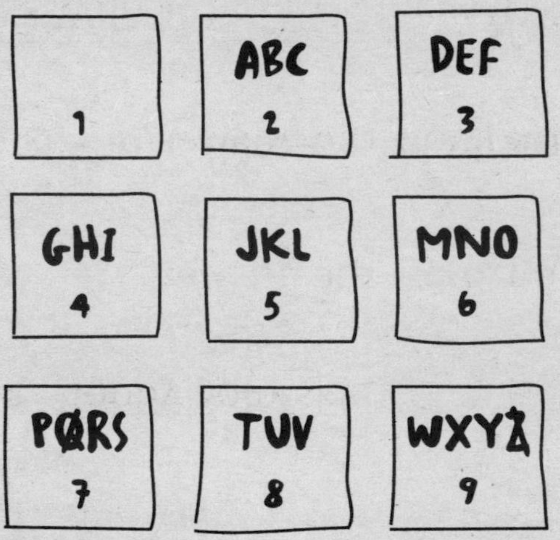

Now comes the tricky part. The number four, for example, has the letters GHI above it. To figure out which letter your partner means, look at the special mark above the number. The letter on the left gets a - (minus) sign. In the middle, a zero. On the right, a + (plus) sign. Can you solve the secret code? Don't forget to cross out the Q and Z.

- 0 + /+ + /- + - + - - + /0 0 + - /+ 0 + 0 0 -

946/47/544729'7/2378/374363?

Answer: ______________________________

Answer: Who is Jigsaw's best friend?

Do you know the answer?

Answer: ______________________________

Answer: Mila Yeh

IPPY Code

Here's another easy one. All you have to do is add the letters IP after every consonant in each word. So the word DOG becomes DIPOGIP and BIGS becomes BIPIGIPSIP. To decode it, all your partner has to do is cross out all the IP's.

Try putting your codebreaking skills to the test. Use the IPPY code to solve this riddle:

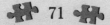

Why was the belt arrested?

FIPORIP HIPOLIPDIPINIPGIP UPIP TIPHIPE PIPANIPTIPSIP!

Answer: ______________________________

Answer: For holding up the pants!

Try writing your own message in the IPPY code below:

____

____

Vowel Code

The five vowels are A, E, I, O, and U. When you use a vowel code, you switch the vowels a little. The vowel *A* in the real word becomes *E* in the code word. *E* becomes *I, I* becomes *O, O* becomes *U,* and *U* becomes *A.*

Du yua git ot?

Answer: ______________________________

Answer: Do you get it?

Try writing your partner a message in vowel code:

If they can crack the code, ask them to write you a coded message back!

Clockwise Box Code

Clockwise box code messages are written in the shape of a box. To read them, start from the top left corner and go around like a clock. The message ends when you wind your way to the middle. It might seem tricky at first, but once you get the hang of it, you can use it to send lots of secret messages!

See if you can read the clockwise box code message on the next page. Does it sound familiar?

F O R A D O
E P R O B L
K W A Y L L
A A . E A
M O G S M R
E W Y A D A

Answer: ______________________________

Answer: For a dollar a day we make problems go away.

Crease Code

Before you start writing your message, fold your paper into thirds. Then unfold it. There should be two long crease marks across the page. Only the letters written across the crease marks matter in this code. So you can write whatever you want on the page, as long as the letters running down the crease marks spell out your secret message. See if you can crack the crease code on the next page.

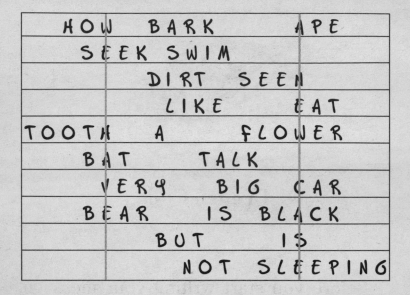

HOW BARK APE
SEEK SWIM
DIRT SEEN
LIKE EAT
TOOTH A FLOWER
BAT TALK
VERY BIG CAR
BEAR IS BLACK
BUT IS
NOT SLEEPING

Can you figure out the code?

Answer: ______________________________

Answer: We have a new case

Grocery List Code

Mila invented this code herself. She almost stumped Jigsaw! But he figured it out eventually. Can you?

4 marshmallows
6 coffee cups
3 coconuts
6 peppers
4 blueberries
4 tarts

1 cookie
3 spoons
3 TV dinners
2 lemons

Here's the trick. The numbers hold the key. The first item on the list is "4 marshmallows." So count to the fourth letter of that word: "s." For "6 coffee cups," count to the sixth letter: "e." Each item is code for one letter. When you put them all together, what do you get? A "SECRET CODE"!

Up-and-Down Code

Most messages are written across, from left to right. This secret message is written up and down, from bottom to top and then top to bottom. Just start at the bottom of the first column, read up, then go over to the next column and read down, then over, then up again.

Use the up-and-down code to figure out this riddle:

What did the beach say when the tide came in?

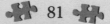

G T E A
N I S
OMO
L E N

Answer: ______________________________

Answer: Long time no sea

Space code

This code is one of the simplest in the business. All the words are spelled right and in the right order, but the spaces are in the wrong places. So to solve it, all you need to do is figure out where the spaces should be. And if you're the one writing the message, just put the spaces wherever you want.

Try the code on the next page! Can you figure out the answer?

Th iscod eise asyi fyo ukn
ow w hatyo uar edo ing!

Answer: ______________________________

Answer: This code is easy if you know what you are doing!

Now write a space code of your own:

____

____

Tic-tac-toe Code

This code is sort of like making your own secret alphabet. Here is the letter key:

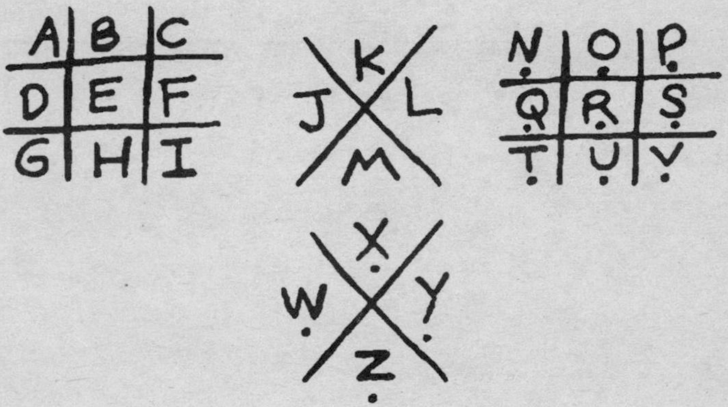

The alphabet for the code comes from the letter key like this:

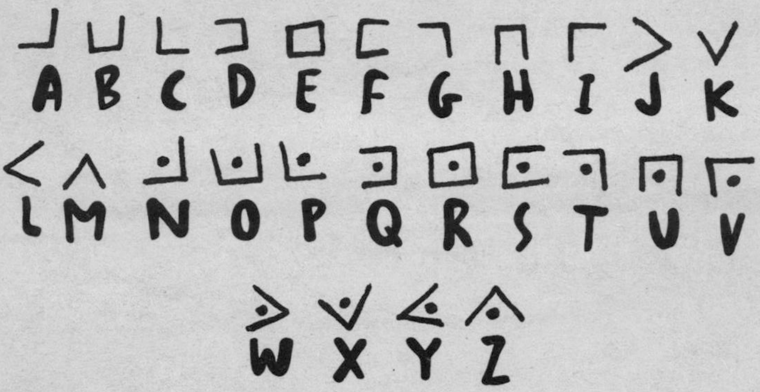

Try writing your name in your new secret language:

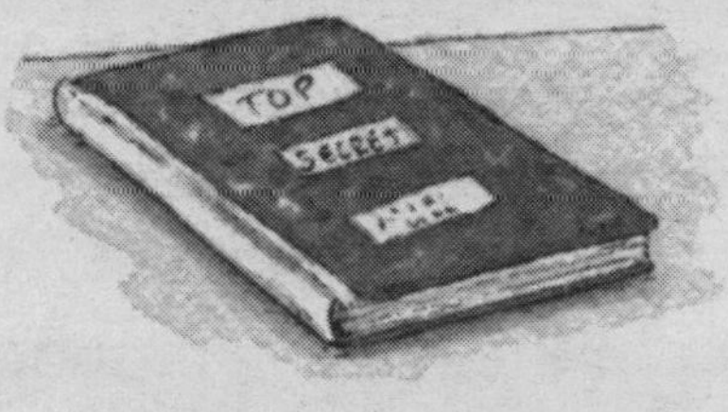

Morse Code

With Morse code, you can send messages using sound or light. Your coded message is made up of dots and dashes. Here is the key:

A .-	J .- - -	S ...
B -...	K -.-	T -
C -.-.	L .-..	U ..-
D -..	M - -	V ...-
E .	N -.	W.- -
F ..-.	O - - -	X -..-
G - -.	P .- -.	Y -.- -
H	Q - -.-	Z - -..
I ..	R .-.	

You can write down the dots and dashes for your partner. But you can also send a message using a flashlight. (This is a good code for sending messages over long distances, or in the dark.) For a dot, turn the light on and off quickly. For a dash, turn it on for a longer time. Just make sure you pause between each letter, so your partner has time to decode the message.

Write your secret message here!

____

____

____

Mini Mysteries

Put Your New Skills to the Test

Now you have almost everything you need to be a great detective. There's just one thing you're missing: experience. Before you start solving cases of your own, why not get some practice? Jigsaw and Mila need your help to solve a few of their toughest cases. So get ready to put your new detective skills to work!

Turn the page to get started, Detective!

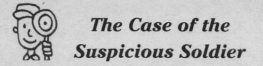

The Case of the Suspicious Soldier

"You have to help me, Jigsaw!" Joey Pignattano said.

You hear that a lot when you're a detective. Lucky for Joey, I was pretty sure I could help. After all, that's my job. For a dollar a day, I make problems go away.

"So what's wrong?" I asked, after Joey paid me. (I always get paid in advance.)

When Joey had found me, I was on the playground, swinging. Now he sank down onto a swing next to me and put his head in his hands.

"It's Bobby Solofsky," he moaned.

Somehow, I wasn't surprised. Whenever there's trouble, you can bet that Bobby's got something to do with it. Trouble is his middle name.

"What'd he do now?" I asked with a groan.

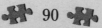

I was getting a little tired of cleaning up Bobby's messes.

"I made this bet," Joey explained. "I was bragging about how I found this box of all my great-grandfather's stuff from World War II. It's really cool, Jigsaw. There are postcards, photos, and even a medal, and —"

"Get to the bet," I urged him. Recess was almost over, and I wanted to earn my dollar.

"Well, everyone thought it was really cool that I had stuff that old. Except Bobby. He claimed he had something even older. But you know Bobby. . . ."

Unfortunately, I did.

"You didn't believe him?" I guessed. "So you bet him that he didn't have anything older?"

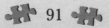

"Yeah." Joey slumped down a little in his seat and shook his head. "Pretty dumb, huh? Because today he came in and brought me this." Joey handed me a tattered postcard. It had a picture of the ocean on the front and a lot of tiny, scraggly handwriting on the back. "He says it's from World War I."

"That definitely came before World War II," I pointed out.

"I know," Joey sighed. "If this postcard is real, it means I lose the bet. And I have to give him my great-grandfather's medal. My mother will kill me!" He turned to look at me with wide, scared eyes. "Jigsaw, you have to help me. You know Bobby — I'm sure this postcard is a fake. I just need your help proving it. Bobby said I could have until the end of recess. And then I have to give him the medal!"

This was serious. I examined the postcard carefully. After all, observation is a detective's best friend. The front photo showed a long, blue stretch of ocean, and that was it. No clues there. The picture could have been taken a hundred years ago . . . or yesterday.

Time was running out.

I turned the postcard over and read the back.

April 31, 1915

My dearest Anna,

It is so hard being away from you and the children. This is a picture of the beach we camped on yesterday. Isn't it beautiful? Someday, maybe we can all come back here together. When World War I is over, we should take a vacation. Until then, I will think of you every night.

Yours,

Robert Solofsky

The postcard was so sweet, it made my teeth hurt. Especially because I knew all that sweetness was fake.

"Good news," I told Joey. "Your medal is

safe. This postcard is about as real as Monopoly money."

How will Jigsaw prove the postcard is a fake?

Answer: The date is an instant giveaway. The postcard is dated April 31 — but April only has thirty days! Also, the soldier calls it "World War I." But no one called it "World War I" until there was a "World War II." If the soldier was really fighting in the first world war, how did he know there was going to be a second one?

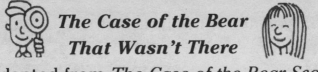

The Case of the Bear That Wasn't There

Adapted from *The Case of the Bear Scare*

Mila and I rushed over to Lucy Hiller's house as soon as she called. I was glad to have an excuse to leave my breakfast table. We were having blueberry pancakes. Blech. I hate blueberries. Grams picked them fresh last season. Then she froze them so we could have blueberries all year long. Lucky me.

When we got to Lucy's, she was home alone. But this wasn't anything like the movie.

"It's just us?" I asked.

"Yeah, just us," Lucy said. "And whoever — or *whatever* — is out there." Lucy pointed through the window at the woods beyond her backyard.

"What are you talking about?" I asked.

"Did you see something out there? Was it a robber?"

"Worse," Lucy answered.

"An animal?" Mila guessed. "Like a big dog or something?"

"Worse," Lucy repeated.

"What could be worse?" I joked. "Did you see Bigfoot tiptoe through the tulips?"

Lucy looked at the carpet. Her face went pale.

"A *bear . . . ?*" Mila guessed.

Lucy slapped a few dollars into Mila's hand. "You got it! *You're* the detectives. What are you waiting for? Start detectin'!"

We all stepped into Lucy's large, sprawling backyard. Tall trees towered above us. The sky was clear and bright. A light breeze blew, carrying with it all the promises of spring.

"Look at this, Jigsaw." Mila held up a wooden pole that had been snapped in half. At the top, there was a birdfeeder.

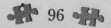

"It would take a chubby squirrel to do that," I quipped.

"Or a bear," Mila stated. "They love birdseed."

I had to admit, it looked suspicious. But we needed something more. We needed proof. That's when we saw it: a pile of bear poop. We had learned about bears in Ms. Gleason's class that week, so we knew just what it should look like. But there was a big difference between seeing it in a book . . . and almost stepping in it.

Funny thing was, it didn't seem gross or anything. It was sort of, um, muddy and leafy, with lots of blueberries mashed up in it. Mila's and Lucy's faces went pale, and they both took a big step back. They looked like they thought a bear was going to come charging out of the woods at any minute.

Mila spoke first. "Here's the proof," she said. "Now let's get inside and call the police."

"Not so fast," I said, as the truth finally hit me. "Lucy, you don't have a bear. You have a prankster."

"What do you mean?" she asked, still looking scared.

"There's no bear," I told her. "It's all a setup." Someone had done a pretty good job of fooling her into thinking there was a bear. But they weren't good enough to fool Jigsaw Jones, ace detective!

How does Jigsaw know the bear wasn't there?

Answer: The "bear poop" had blueberries in it. But blueberries were out of season. (Remember Grams' pancakes!) So it had to be fake.

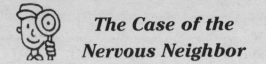

The Case of the Nervous Neighbor

"Quick, hide me, Jigsaw!" Wingnut scrambled up the ladder and threw himself into my tree house. He cowered behind the wall for a minute and looked out nervously. Then he sighed. I guess the coast was clear.

"Are you going to tell me what's going on?" I asked. It's not every day that your next-door neighbor shows up looking like the world is about to end. Though with Wingnut as my neighbor, it has happened more than once.

"You have to make my problem go away," Wingnut pleaded. "Please, Jigsaw!"

"Got a dollar?" I asked. But I already knew what the answer would be.

Wingnut's big flappy ears turned bright red. His nose started to twitch. His eyes started to water. It didn't take a detective to tell he was about to cry.

Yeesh.

"It's okay, Wingnut," I told him. "You can owe me one."

"Thanks, Jigsaw!" He beamed and held out his candy bar. "You can have some of this, if you want."

I snapped off a piece and chomped on it. Mmm. It was sweet and crisp. But the day was so hot that it melted almost as soon as it hit my mouth.

Once we'd chowed down, it was time to get back to business.

"What's the problem, Wingnut?" I asked.

"There's this vase that my mom really loves," he began. His eyes started watering again. "And . . . it broke."

"How did it break?" I asked.

"I don't know!" he yelped. "I swear. I've been outside playing all afternoon. I haven't been inside once."

"So how do you know the vase is

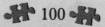

broken?" I asked. A good detective is always suspicious.

"I heard a crash," Wingnut claimed. "Then I looked through the window and saw it broken on the floor. That's when I came here. I just know my mom is going to think I did it!"

"So you want me to figure out who broke the vase?" I summed up for him. I snapped off another piece of the chocolate bar. Even in the last few minutes, it had gotten softer in the hot sun. I decided I better eat it quick before it all disappeared. "Who do you think it was?"

Wingnut fidgeted, and I could see that sweat was pouring down his forehead. Was he hot? Or was he nervous?

"I don't know, Jigsaw," he whined. "That's your job. Maybe a bird flew into the house. Or maybe it was a raccoon. But it wasn't me. It couldn't have been. I was outside all afternoon. I told you."

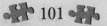

“But if your mom thinks it was you, she’ll probably be really mad,” I guessed. “You’ll be in big trouble, right?”

“Maybe even *grounded,*” Wingnut added in a hushed voice. We both shuddered. “Can you help me?”

“No,” I said. His face fell. “But I can tell you who broke the vase.”

“Who?” Wingnut asked in a tiny voice. He twisted his head over his shoulder as if the culprit were standing behind him.

It was a good thing that Wingnut hadn’t paid me a dollar. Because it hadn’t taken me more than five minutes to solve this case. And he wasn’t going to like the solution very much.

I mashed the rest of the sticky gob of chocolate into my mouth, then pointed to my client.

“Sorry, Wingnut. But the culprit is *you.*”

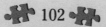

How does Jigsaw know that Wingnut broke the vase?

Answer: The proof is in the chocolate. Wingnut swore that he'd been outside all afternoon. But if that was true, why didn't his chocolate bar melt under the very hot sun? He must have gotten the chocolate bar from inside the house just before he ran to Jigsaw's. The chocolate melted before he could even finish telling Jigsaw about his case. Wingnut had no reason to lie . . . unless he was the one who broke the vase.

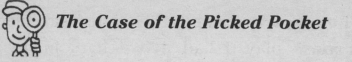

"There is a thief in Room 201," our teacher, Ms. Gleason, announced. She looked pretty mad at us. She also looked pretty disappointed. That part was even worse. Ms. Gleason is probably the nicest teacher ever. We all wanted her to think we were a good class.

And usually, we were.

"Geetha, can you come up here, please?" Ms. Gleason asked. Geetha joined her at the front of the room. She was wearing a cast on her right arm. The week before, she had fallen off her bike and landed on her arm. My arm hurt just thinking about it. Geetha was also wearing a very sad frown. My detective instinct told me that she was the victim of our classroom thief. And I was right.

"Tell the class what happened," Ms. Gleason encouraged her.

"Before we started the rehearsal for our class play, I had five dollars in my pocket," Geetha began. "After the rehearsal, it was gone. Someone must have stolen it!"

"Does anyone know where Geetha's five dollars are?" Ms. Gleason asked sternly.

We all shook our heads. Except Bobby Solofsky. He raised his hand like he wanted to help. Behind me, I heard Mila sigh. When Bobby tries to "help," things usually get worse. Make that *always*.

"Ms. Gleason, I have a suspect," Bobby said loudly.

The class gasped. We held our breath to hear him say the name.

"I think that it was Ralphie Jordan!" Bobby said. Everyone gasped again and looked over at Ralphie.

"Was not!" Ralphie shouted, standing up at his desk. He looked even madder than Ms. Gleason.

“Calm down, class,” our teacher warned us. “Bobby, tell us why you think that.”

“They were standing in a row on the end of the stage during rehearsal. Athena, Helen, Geetha, and then Ralphie. And they were singing that dumb — uh, I mean, that nice song.”

I knew exactly what scene in the play he was talking about. Athena, Helen, Geetha, and Ralphie were in the front row of the chorus. They were supposed to sing a song about vegetables, while the rest of us danced around the stage. For the actual show, we would all have to dress up in vegetable costumes. I was going to be a kumquat. I’d never even *seen* a kumquat, and now I had to be one. Yeesh.

“Ralphie was right next to Geetha,” Bobby continued. “While Geetha was singing, I suspect that Ralphie stuck his hand in her pocket and pulled out the money. She didn’t even notice.”

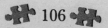

Ms. Gleason frowned.

"He's lying!" Ralphie cried. "I didn't do anything. I didn't!"

That's when I raised my hand. Usually, I charge a dollar a day to make problems go away. But in this case, I was willing to do it for free. Something sounded pretty fishy about Bobby's detective work. And it was going to take a *real* detective to figure out what.

"Ms. Gleason, can I ask Bobby a question?" I asked. I tried my best to look like a serious detective.

"Yes, Jigsaw. If you think you can help us get to the bottom of this," she said.

"Was Ralphie standing to Geetha's right, or to her left?" I asked.

Bobby stopped to think for a second, and then he grinned. "He was on her right," he replied. "I remember because he almost knocked over that giant carrot on the end of the stage. That was funny." Bobby started

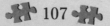

laughing, but I knew that I was about to wipe the smile off his face in a hurry.

"Ms. Gleason, I don't know what happened to Geetha's money," I said. "But Ralphie is innocent — and I can prove it!"

How will Jigsaw prove that Ralphie is not the thief?

Answer: If Ralphie were standing on Geetha's right side, the money would have to be in Geetha's right pocket. But Geetha has a cast on her right arm. She wouldn't have been able to put her money into that pocket. So it must have been in her left pocket. Bobby was trying to be a top detective, but he missed a very important fact!

From the Top Secret Pages of Jigsaw Jones's Detective Journal

Now you can solve mysteries like Jigsaw Jones and Mila Yeh!

Case: The case of ______________________

Client: ______________________

Suspects: ______________________

____

Clues: ______________________

____

Key words: ______________________

____

Mystery Solved: ______________________

____

From the Top Secret Pages of Jigsaw Jones's Detective Journal

Now you can solve mysteries like Jigsaw Jones and Mila Yeh!

Case: The case of ______________________________

Client: ______________________________

Suspects: ______________________________

____

Clues: ______________________________

____

Key words: ______________________________

____

Mystery Solved: ______________________________

____